Heroes in Headlines

Vol. 1

Bringing the past to life TODAY

Ancient Stories

in Modern Historical Headlines©

by

Joseph Patrick Cosgrove

Joseph's Dream News©

For information email
heroesinheadlines@yahoo.com

Published by Golden Additions
Las Vegas, NV
Printed in United States of America

Edited by Janet Cosgrove

ISBN 978-0-9893549-2-9

ISBN 978-0-9893549-3-6 (e-book)

You can bring the author to your live event as an inspirational speaker. For information email

heroesinheadlines@yahoo.com

Library of Congress Control Number:
2013951918

https://www.facebook.com/HeroesinHeadlines

www.heroesinheadlines.com

Illustrations by Jeffrey K. Bedrick
www.JeffreykBedrick.com

Cover layout by
Joel Christopher Payne
www.joelfineart.com

Previous Publications by
Joseph Patrick Cosgrove
Walt Dreamers Me© 2013

Watch for future

Heroes in Headlines©

A unique Series of Books
Bringing the past to life

Moses News

Prince in Egypt, Freedom Fighter

Jesus News

Greatest good news story in human history

Benjamin Franklin News

The only Founding Father in the
Swimmer's Hall of Fame

Thomas Jefferson News

Author of the Declaration of Independence

John Adams News

Voice of the Declaration of Independence

George Washington News

America's first President and
Commander in Chief

And *Synchronicity,* the autobiography
of Joseph Patrick Cosgrove

TABLE OF CONTENTS

CHAPTER 1 *THE STORY BEGINS*   **1**

CHAPTER 3 *JOSEPH REMAINS*   **23**

FAITHFUL   **23**

CHAPTER 4 *DREAM INTERPRETATIONS*   **29**

CHAPTER 5 *PROMOTION TIME*   **37**

CHAPTER 6 *REUNION*   **45**

CHAPTER 7 *JOSEPH REVEALED*   **57**

CHAPTER 8 *THE PLAN*   **65**

CHAPTER 9 *THE END OF AN ERA*   **69**

FUTURE EPILOGUE HEADLINES: **74**

EPILOGUE   **76**

Special Acknowledgements

To our friends have who assisted in any way
with the Bible Series

Heroes In Headlines©

JOSEPH'S DREAM NEWS©2013

I truly thank you

The Davidsohn Corporation;

Tod, Josh and Nick Ulery,

The Jewelry Box of Campbell, CA;

Brad & Michelle Rocca, Original Joe's, San Jose,
CA;

Mike Fica

DEDICATION

With fond memories and a heart full of gratitude I dedicate the Bible story series of *Heroes in Headlines* to Wheaton College, Wheaton, Illinois and Fuller Theological Seminary, Pasadena, California.

A special remembrance and gratitude goes to the following:

Dr. V. Raymond Edman, President of Wheaton College(1940-1965), who took special interest in me and was a lifelong inspiration; "Papa" Louis Rasera and his family who were my family during my college years;

Dr. Russell Mixter, Dr. Richey Kamm, Dr. Earnest Larson and Dr. Earl Cairns, who opened new worlds of knowledge and expanded my world; and

Dean of Students Arthur Volle who was patient with my campus pranks and musical mayhem on campus as the Head Cheerleader at Wheaton.

Ancient Headlines

Ancient Front Page Headlines have flowed from my imagination, knowledge and research.

This is my effort to represent ancient stories in a modern newspaper or popular magazine style of reporting for the modern reader who may have a shorter attention span and little knowledge of ancient past, or of epistemology, psychology, cosmology, theology, astronomy, science, psycholinguistics, politics and religion.

By presenting these ancient stories using modern idioms and formats we make them come alive in dealing with real life problems, challenges and circumstances in the world today.

In ancient characters we can learn something about life today and about ourselves.

Is it possible to see the repeat of history as you read through these headlines? History will show you the future if you understand and gain perspectives from studying narratives of the past.

Joseph Patrick Cosgrove

JOSEPH'S

REINVENTED LIFE

Presented as Volume One

in a series from

Heroes in

Headlines©

Joseph's Dream News

A Journey from

Slavery and Prison

to

Ruler of Egypt

INTRODUCTION

The legendary Patriarch of the opening book of the Bible, Genesis, is Abraham who had many children, including Joseph's father Jacob. Joseph is the 11th son of Jacob and his wife Rachel. In ancient Hebrew the name Joseph means "God increases."

Our Cover Story of Joseph's heroic adventures is the timeless tale of a young person who faces many challenges while growing up and how he responds and reacts to these challenges.

Joseph Campbell states that these ancient Biblical stories are about the "hero's journey." Campbell defines a hero as someone who has given his or her life to something bigger than oneself.

The root definition of the word "hero" means "to protect and to serve" something Joseph does during his entire life.

Joseph is still celebrated in pop culture through Andrew Lloyd Webber and Tim Rice in *Joseph and the Amazing Technicolor Dream Coat,* a musical stage and film production experienced by millions of people worldwide.

CHAPTER 1 *THE STORY BEGINS*

JOSEPH,
JACOB'S SON OF HIS OLD AGE

Joseph is the youngest son of Rachel and Jacob.

The Patriarch Jacob has several wives but Rachel is the love of his life.

Jacob shows obvious preferential treatment to Joseph because he is the son of his old age.

JACOB CREATES
UNINTENDED CONSEQUENCES

The Patriarch Jacob, also known as Israel, loves all his sons but focuses considerable attention on his young son Joseph. This causes dismay and resentment with his other sons.

Jacob wants only the very best for Joseph but his favoritism stirs up a hornet's nest of jealousy and hatred among Joseph's brothers.

BROTHER'S RESENT
UNEQUAL TREATMENT

Joseph's brothers resent their father's ongoing special treatment of their spoiled little brat sibling.

Jacob loves little Joseph a lot but his brothers despise their younger brother. Jacob's pampering of Joseph has ignited a growing sibling rivalry.

JACOB'S GIFT BACKFIRES

On his 17th birthday Joseph receives a custom made garment from his doting Father, Jacob. Jacob's special birthday gift stirs up more resentment from Joseph's brothers who continuously taunt him at every op.

The gift, a carefully tailored colorful coat has set Joseph up as a highly desirable and despicable moving target for abuse by his jealous older brothers.

RADIANT RAGS RANKLE RABBLE ROUSING RELATIVES

Jacob has always been overly attentive to his youngest son Joseph. Jacob has

Joseph dressed up in a glitzy phantasmagoria coat of many colors.

Jacob's gift sets Joseph apart from his down in the dumps dressed hillbilly sheepherding brothers who are colored green with envy. Joseph's new coat is stirring up more disputes and problems between Joseph and his brothers.

JACOB'S FAMILY FEUD

Sibling rivalry erupts in the Land of Canaan in the household of the famous Patriarch Jacob and his 12 sons.

Joseph is Jacob's eyes and ears on what is happening in the work place among family members. Joseph is truthful and often tells his father of some of the bad things his half-brothers are doing. Joseph's eavesdropping is dramatically inflaming the tension between Joseph and his brothers. Some of Joseph's brothers are even threatening him with bodily harm.

JACOB'S YOUNG PROTÉGÉ

Joseph is Jacobs's closest son and as such has learned a great deal about his father's business, starting with tending his father's flocks of livestock to working as a farm hand in the fields of grain.

Joseph assists his father Jacob by taking on many logistical responsibilities for him. Joseph is a hustler eager to serve his family.

His brothers greatly resent their father's favoritism to Joseph, causing a deep rift between father and sons.

BIG DREAMER ROCKS FAMILY

Patriarch Jacob's young son Joseph is noted for his futuristic dreams.

He excitedly tells his 11 brothers about his latest dream. According to the dream all Jacobs's sons were in a field binding up sheaves, Joseph says, "and when my sheaf stood up all your sheaves gathered around and bowed very low to it."

The brother's response was instantaneous. "You see yourself ruling over us," they said with sneering smiles, negatively shaking heads and waving fists. The brother's hatred for Joseph has boiled over because of his dreams and his superior attitude.

FURIOUS FALLOUT FOLLOWS

The older brothers continue to deride Joseph with taunts and insults about his fantastic futuristic dreams of his superiority over them.

Joseph's brothers feel he is trying to denigrate them and make them lose face with their father.

Joseph continues to have dreams about his family's future and his family continues to dislike them.

SKYHIGH DREAMS SHOCK ALL

Joseph has once again told family members about his latest out of this world dream which forecasts a future event when "The sun, the moon and eleven stars bow low before me."

Jacob asks Joseph, "Does this dream mean your mother and brothers come and bow low to you?" "The future is what I say it is" Joseph states.

While Joseph's brothers continue to harass him for his dreams, Jacob has paused to ponder the true meaning of Joseph's reoccurring dreams. Joseph's dreams are his brother's worst nightmare for they cannot ever imagine bowing down before him under any circumstances. Joseph believes his dreams are inspired by his faith in God and are a forecast of his future.

JOSEPH'S PASSIONATE DREAMS

Joseph's dreams are storyboarding images of his life's purpose and goals. Joseph visualizes in his imagination that God is with him every day no matter what is happening to him. Joseph believes God has a higher calling for his life and his faith keeps him purpose driven every day.

Joseph's faith and trust in God is the driving source of his guiding principles of integrity, honesty, service to others and human dignity.

JOSEPH AND HIS BROTHERS ARE ON COLLISION COURSE

Joseph's feisty brothers move the family flocks to Shechem to vast open fields ripe for grazing their sheep and goats.

While on the road, Joseph's jealous and paranoid brother's hatch rampageous plans to get rid of their cocky little brother Joe who they contend is just a snitch for their father.

Some want to harm him while others just want to intimidate him physically. The plot becomes a mean spirited encounter for their spying little brother the next time he shows up to check on them.

JOSEPH DEPARTS VALLEY

The youngest son of Jacob leaves Hebron today to Shechem on another mission by his father, the Patriarch Jacob.

Joseph is sent to assess the progress of his brothers and family flocks feeding in Shechem. Jacob has requested a detailed report on how the brothers are getting along as well as the condition of the flocks.

SEARCHING AT SHECHEM

Joseph, youngest son of Jacob, arrives in Shechem looking for his family. After hiking the area Joseph finds no trace of his brothers and the family flocks.

After hours of looking Joseph finally encounters a local resident who informs him his brothers and their flocks left days ago for Dothan.

Joseph picks up their trail and sets out to follow them.

BULLIES BASH BROTHER

From afar Joseph is seen wearing his coat of many colors as he approaches, while his brothers, with malice aforethought, get ready to give him a very hard time. Joseph's coat has made him a target for their collective frustrations and feelings of being thought inferior by their brother's outrageous big shot dreams.

"Here comes the big dreamer boy, let's kill him and toss his body into a well," someone shouts. "Yeah, then we shall see what happens to all his stupid dreams!" another says angrily.

Upon arriving in Dothan Joseph is surrounded, overwhelmed and pushed around by his 11 brothers. His brightly colored coat is stripped off of him with gleeful delight by his jealous siblings.

A PROMPT INTERVENTION

"Let's not kill him," Jacob's oldest son Reuben shouts to his co-conspirators, "Let's not shed blood, let us throw him into this deep well and he will die without our touching him."

Elder brother Reuben, fearing for Joseph's life, is plotting to free Joseph from the dry well as soon as he can as he watches Joseph tossed into the well.

CRIES FOR HELP FROM WELL

Local shepherds report hearing echoing calls for help from deep down a long dry well in Shechem.

Patriarch Jacob's sons say the sounds are imaginary audio mirages over stimulated by drinking too much wine after dark.

7

BROTHER'S SCHEME BARED

Upon seeing an Ishmaelite caravan coming their way, Judah bellows to his brothers, "Hey guys, I have a great idea! Let's sell Joseph to them. I agree with Ruben why kill Joseph and have his death on our conscience."

All his brothers agree to the quick sale while Reuben is away on an errand.

JOSEPH PULLED FROM WELL

Joseph is hoisted out of the deep dry well by his brothers who have concocted a devious plan for him.

A confused Joseph is cleaned up by his hostile brothers who are selling him as a slave to make some money.

JOSEPH SALE = SILVER SHEKELS

Joseph's brothers earn a quick profit by removing Joseph from the deep well and selling him to passing Ishmaelite traders for twenty shekels of silver.

The brothers are now cooking up a fantasy tale for Jacob about his son Joseph being a bright new star in the heavens above.

JOSEPH'S JOURNEY JOLTS

Now a captive of slave traders, Joseph is being carried away into an unknown destination and future. His family ties resonate with each mile that separates him from his roots. Will he ever see his father again? How could his brothers do this?

Homesickness floods his being as his journey to an unknown future continues. What will become of him? His life is being changed forever and his future is uncertain. He remains comforted by the thought of the faithfulness of the God of Abraham, Isaac and his father Jacob. No matter what, God is always near is Joseph's firm belief.

MOB MENTALITY
MORPHS MALEVOLENT

The band of brothers' mob mentality goes out of control as they vent their anger by ripping and tearing apart Joseph's colorful coat.

They all agree to make up a cover story to convince their father that his missing son was killed by a wild animal.

REUBEN'S DISPAIR

Reuben returns to the well only to find to his surprise that Joseph is gone. Confronting his brothers, he cries out that Joseph is missing from the well.

Heartbroken Reuben falls to the ground as he is filled with angst and frustration when confronted with the bloody clothing.

JOSEPH HAS VANISHED

Joseph was sent to check on the brothers' work and report back to his father on their whereabouts and progress.

Joseph's failure to return home has stressed out Jacob who expresses growing concern about his son's strange disappearance. It is not like Joseph; his father says to his wife, something is terribly wrong.

JOSEPH REPORTED AS KILLED

In a cover up scheme Joseph's brothers have splattered their missing brother's torn and tattered shirt with goat's blood. Joseph's brothers produce a blood soaked coat of many colors to their father asking him, "Is this Joseph's coat?"

After viewing the bloody garment, Jacob falls to the ground, overwhelmed by the thought of his son Joseph being torn to pieces by wild animals. "Yes," Jacob sobbed, "this is my son's coat. Joseph has been killed."

JACOB'S MELTDOWN

Joseph has now been proclaimed dead for weeks, causing trauma and turmoil in the House of Jacob. Jacob is trying to come to terms with his loss of a beloved son.

Jacob has hit rock bottom and is in a deep depression over his missing son. The aging Patriarch's emotional life has been upended by his son's death. He hurts deeply and his body is in shock as he has not slept in days.

JACOB IS UNDONE

Eye witnesses state Jacob has fallen into a crushing emotional collapse at the reports of little Joe's death. Jacob is in seclusion to deal with his grief.

"I will die mourning for my son," cries a tearful inconsolable Jacob. The brothers' efforts to console him are of no avail as Jacob has fallen into a slough of despair over the loss of Joseph.

JOSEPH ON SLAVE BLOCK

The Ishmaelite slave trader is touting Joseph's good looks, intelligence, farming skills and dream interpretation to get the highest possible price.

Lively bidding is expected for this young man from Israel assuring a high financial return for the Ishmaelite slave trader.

A DIAMOND IN THE ROUGH

Today, Potiphar, powerful and wealthy member of Pharaoh's personal staff and Chief of Security, purchases Joseph, missing son of Jacob the Patriarch. The Hebrew slave will now serve in the household of one of the most powerful families in Egypt.

Potiphar, a good judge of men, states he sees potential in the handsome young man. Potiphar outbids many others in order to be the owner of the first Hebrew ever put on sale in Egypt.

JOSEPH A TOP PERFORMER

Potiphar, Captain of Pharaoh's body guards, says Joseph, his newly purchased Hebrew slave, is very diligent in fulfilling all his responsibilities.

Potiphar states he feels The Almighty God is blessing Joseph in a very special way.

Joseph is already handling many more assignments for Pharaoh's Chief of Security.

JOSEPH'S CULTURE SHOCK

Joseph, the Hebrew slave, finds himself in the house of Potiphar, a powerful member of Pharaoh's elite inner circle. He is now immersed in a land where polytheism dominates.

Joseph is surrounded by people who strongly believe in the afterlife.

MANY GODS THRIVE IN EGYPT

Joseph is confronted with the unfamiliar world of Egypt's Gods of Nature such as Ben-Ben, Nun, Geb and Nut. Egyptians believe these deities will make fields of crops fertile, healthy and flourishing thereby preventing famine.

The fresh faced boy from a small village named Hebron is now facing big city life in Egypt as well as its omni-present Parthenon of ancient Gods.

PHARAOH IS A LIVING GOD

Pharaoh is Egypt's living God and rules over a theocracy of many Gods.

Pharaoh governs with the cooperation of his cronies, the priests of Horus, to prevent famine and to promote social harmony.

The God Sobek is a symbol of Pharaoh's frightening power.

SNARKY CROCK SYMBOLIZES SOBEK

Egypt is totally dependent upon the water of the Nile River and regular seasonal rainfall for the enrichment of its agriculturally based economy. Egyptians fear the Nile's many crocodiles and worship the Nile God Sobek to seek his protection while traveling on the Nile's crocodile infested waters.

JOSEPH ANCHORS HIS BEHAVIOR

Egypt equates all its Gods with nature, sun, wind, earth, sky and animals. Surrounded by the many Gods of Egypt, Joseph remains steadfast in his belief of only one God, one morality and the sanctity of human life.

Joseph remains grounded in his belief that there is only one God who is above nature and all of creation.

BELIEFS BACKSTOP BEHAVIOR

Joseph's faith is in a God who demands of him that he behave decently towards other people. Joseph prays and worships only one God of heaven and earth.

He believes God has created us all in His image thereby making human life sacred. He also believes the Source of his existence has purpose for his life. Joseph seeks God's guidance for his daily life.

JOSEPH NAMED MAJOR DOMO

The well-known Chief of Pharaoh's secret service, Potiphar, announces today the appointment of Joseph as head of all his household affairs.

Under Potiphar, Joseph has grown and demonstrated strong management and organizational skills and has become invaluable to his new mentor, the Chief of Egypt's Security forces.

JOSEPH GETS PROMOTION

Potiphar announces the appointment of the Hebrew slave Joseph as head of operations for all of his business affairs.

Potiphar and Joseph have bonded over the years and the young Hebrew is now a strong right-hand man. The two enjoy mutual trust and confidence, making for a special partnership.

POTIPHAR EMPIRE FLOURISHES

During the past several years Potiphar's farm crops and livestock have dramatically increased under the control and management of young Joseph.

Some insiders feel the favor of God is upon Potiphar because of Joseph, a Hebrew slave who believes one God, the Creator of all, exists. Potiphar has put his faith in Joseph because of his virtues of honesty, loyalty, and trustworthiness.

POTIPHAR'S RISING STAR

Egypt's Chief Law Enforcement person, Potiphar, is spending more time serving Pharaoh now that his household and agricultural operations are being managed by the new rising star named Joseph.

Potiphar is spending more of his time with Pharaoh much to the delight of the nation's ruler.

Potiphar reveals new plans for the nation's prison system as well as for additional security for Pharaoh's household.

POTIPHAR'S WIFE STALKS JOSEPH

In addition to tending to his master's household chores, Joseph has become an object of the affection of Mrs. Potiphar, a member of the self-absorbed Cheating Wives Club of Egypt.

Cradle-robbing Mrs. Potiphar acts like a passion puppy excitedly following Joseph around as he handles household matters. Joseph has become her all-consuming obsession and she is demanding his attention for her every need to keep him close at hand.

JOSEPH RESISTS BEING BOY TOY

Joseph tries to avoid the lusting wife of Potiphar who has fallen for him.

Confronting Mrs. Potiphar, Joseph says he will not betray his God or her husband. "Your husband trusts me with everything and I cannot do this wicked thing you ask. It would be a great sin against God." Joseph firmly believes that what matters to God is goodness.

The narcissistic Mrs. Potiphar does not give up easily and continues her romantic pursuit of her husband's right hand man. Self-absorbed she feels Joseph should accommodate her; after all he is her slave.

PERSISTANT SPOUSE
DOES DRAMATIC POUTS

The lovely and charming Mrs. Potiphar has recently taken to long bouts of heavy drinking.

The nation's leading hostess with the mostess is reportedly in a tiff over her failure to captivate her household's handsome dashing dandy who is resisting her flirtiest advances.

The war of romance and roses continues according to eye witnesses. The more Joseph resists her the more she desires him.

UPSET WIFE FEIGNS SCREAM

Mrs. Potiphar is upset with Joseph for not paying attention to her so she plans revenge for his constant resistance to her charms.

Domestic violence flares at the house of Potiphar as Joseph resists Potiphar's wife's overt advances and flees the house while she feigns hysterical screams for help.

In his haste, Joseph leaves behind telltale evidence in the hands of Mrs. Potiphar. The lusty wife had hold of Joseph's shirt and held on to it as he tried to resist her passionate advances.

Eye witnesses report that the wife of the nation's top law enforcement officer was hysterical when household servants found her this morning.

"The Hebrew slave tried to force foul play upon me but when I screamed he ran away but forgot his shirt," she said trembling and crying.

JOSEPH ARRESTED FOR ASSAULT

Mrs. Potiphar tells her husband that his favorite Hebrew slave, Joseph tried to have his way with her but luckily she was able to fight him off.

An angry Potiphar has Joseph taken into custody and chained to a wall in jail with the false charges from Mrs. Potiphar.

WIFE ACCUSES JOSEPH

Jacob's young son is jailed for foul play and will be put on trial.

Joseph is locked up in the national Egyptian prison in the castle of Potiphar while his garments remain under lock and key as evidence of his alleged attempt at foul play.

Potiphar's wife's medical records are sealed due to her status.

POTIPHARS WIFE BEARS ALL

The sobbing wife of Potiphar says Joseph wanted to lie down with her even though she resisted him as she gives her testimony of the event.

She states when she called for help, Joseph ran away leaving his shirt behind in the bedroom. The garment has been offered as evidence of the attack.

It is a "he said, she said" conundrum but with the status of Potiphar's wife, Joseph is sentenced to prison.

POTIPHAR DOUBTS WIFE

The nation's chief law officer has growing doubts about his wife's flapdoodle charges against Joseph. It just runs contrary to everything Joseph believes, especially his faith in God to always do what is morally right and decent.

Potiphar is very familiar with the goings on with some of the famous housewives of Egypt who have too much time on their hands.

Insiders say Potiphar has already made plans to make good use of Joseph's talents while he is serving time in prison in order to make Joseph's time behind bars easier.

CHAPTER 3 *JOSEPH REMAINS FAITHFUL*

GOD REMAINS WITH JOSEPH

It appears that the favor of God continues with the young Hebrew slave Joseph who is currently locked up behind bars. The Chief Jailer makes Joseph his administrative assistant.

Conditions inside the prison improve greatly under Joseph's leadership, much to the delight of the Chief Jailer.

At the urging of Potiphar, the Chief Jailer has put the entire prison administration into the hands of Joseph.

JOSEPH STANDS OUT IN JAIL

The Chief Jailor reports that under Joseph's management the prison administration and operations are working at maximum efficiency compared to the hectic ways of before Joseph.

Behind the scenes, Potiphar, ever the diplomat, keeps in close touch with Joseph. Meanwhile Joseph continues to put his trust and faith in the God of his fathers. This provides him with great comfort as he remains behind prison walls. Somehow, someway, Joseph believes God has a purpose for his life. He cannot even imagine what it might be.

Events continue to unfold in Egypt as Joseph remains totally unaware of their possible impact upon his future.

BUTLER AND BAKER JAILED

An angry and suspicious Pharaoh has ordered the immediate arrest of two of his servants, the Royal Baker and Royal Butler/ Wine Taster.

In developing news, two of Pharaoh's closest servants are found to be persons of interest in a major scandal at the Royal Palace. Both men are confined in Potiphar's jail.

Rumors are overheard as they fly around the countryside about a death plot against Pharaoh. Security is dramatically increased at the Royal Palace.

JOSEPH'S HIGH LEVEL PRISONERS

Egypt's chief law enforcement officer, Potiphar, has assigned his top prison administrator, Joseph, to keep special watch over the jailed baker and butler of the Royal household. Joseph is to report to Potiphar if these two talk about any death plots of Pharaoh.

Suddenly, behind prison bars, Joseph now has a connection to Pharaoh himself through these two most personal servants.

ROYAL SERVANTS STRESSED

A confidential report reveals that Pharaoh's two jailed servants are frequently seen meeting with Joseph.

It is said both men state they have dreams and are concerned about the meaning of them. They are reported stressed out because of not knowing what these dreams might mean. The imprisoned Royal servants have no idea that Joseph can interpret the meaning of dreams.

Joseph assures them that interpreting dreams is something he does with God's help. By interpreting their dreams, Joseph thinks that this just might open the door to freedom for him for they have direct personal contact with Pharaoh himself.

WINE TASTER'S DREAM REVEAL

The Royal wine taster is first to reveal his dream to Joseph.

He states that in his dream he sees a vine with three branches that begin to bud and blossom. Soon there are clusters of ripe grapes. Since I am holding Pharaoh's wine cup in my hand I just squeeze the grapes into juice and hand it to him to drink.

He pleads with Joseph to interpret what this strange dream means.

WINE TASTER WILL BE SET FREE

Potiphar's top jail administrator demonstrates his ability to interpret the Royal Butler's dream during an emotional meeting.

Joseph's interpretation of the wine tasters dream forecasts that in three days Pharaoh will release him from jail and restore him to service in the Royal Palace. A sigh of relief comes from the Royal Butler who is profoundly moved by Joseph's message.

JOSEPH'S PRISON PLEA

Joseph earnestly requests that the wine taster remember him when he is freed from jail.

"When you are back in favor with Pharaoh, ask him to release me. I was kidnapped from my homeland and I am now in jail when I did nothing wrong."

The Butler assures Joseph that he will speak to Pharaoh on his behalf as soon as possible.

BAKER HOPES FOR FREEDOM

As the Royal Baker hears about the happy ending for the Wine Taster's dream he is anxious to share his own dream with Joseph.

The baker tells Joseph, "In my dream I carry three baskets of fresh bakery items on my head for Pharaoh. On the top basket are special pastries made just for Pharaoh. Suddenly birds swoop down and eat them all."

Encouraged by Joseph's interpretation of the wine taster's dream the Royal Baker of Pharaoh is hopeful for similar results.

BAKER'S DEAD END DREAM

Pharaoh's Royal Baker falls into a state of shock and despair as Joseph interprets his dream.

Joseph explains the meaning of the Baker's dream as follows: "The three baskets mean three days. In three days Pharaoh will behead you and impale your body on a pole. Birds will swoop down and pick off your flesh."

The Royal Baker pales as he listens to Joseph's interpretation of his dream. He listens but hopes and prays Joseph is wrong.

PHARAOH'S BIRTHDAY BASH

Three days after Joseph predicts their release from jail, the Butler and Baker are back in the Royal Palace to serve at a Royal Birthday celebration.

Even as they are being released from jail, Joseph prays fervently that the Butler will remember to speak to Pharaoh on his behalf.

JOSEPH'S REAL PREDICTIONS

Events have unfolded exactly as Joseph saw them in the dreams of Pharaoh's two servants.

Both the wine taster and baker have been released from prison in the three days' time to meet their fate as Joseph has forecast.

The Butler has been restored to being official wine taster for Pharaoh while the Baker has been sentenced to be executed in the manner Joseph has predicted.

BUTLER'S MEMORY LOSS

Once back in service to the Pharaoh, the Royal Butler never gives Joseph another thought. Even though he had promised to mention Joseph's injustice he is too caught up in the day to day ceremonies at the Royal Palace and the horrible memories of his time behind bars. He has totally deleted Joseph from his mind.

JOSEPH REMAINS OPTIMISTIC

It has been two years since the wine tasters release and Joseph realizes he has been totally forgotten in jail.

It is very clear that Joseph's plea for mercy and freedom fell on deaf ears. This was not the first time his pleas for justice were ignored. Still his faith in God motivates Joseph to continue serving his fellow man even from behind prison bars. Joseph remains optimistic while being held captive.

PHARAOH'S STRANGE DREAMS

Pharaoh is restless and unsettled. It is reported the Royal Court is in turmoil as Pharaoh is frustrated about uncertain meanings of his recurring and relentless dreams.

The Royal Court is filled with speculation about Pharaoh's recent mind boggling nightmares.

Royal wizards and sages are perplexed and unable to provide a definitive interpretation. Pharaoh continues to seek answers for his reoccurring nightmares. "Who can interpret my dreams" he would often ask during the day even of his servants.

ROYAL BUTLER REMEMBERS

While listening to Pharaoh, the Butler suddenly remembers his promise to Joseph. He remembers while in prison two years ago a Hebrew slave named Joseph had explained his dreams.

Everything the slave, Joseph, had predicted to him in prison has come to pass. He ashamedly recalls his promise to speak to Pharaoh on Joseph's behalf.

CHIEF BUTLER SPEAKS UP

Suddenly the butler tells Pharaoh what happened when he and the Royal Baker were in prison a couple of years ago. How one night both he and the baker had strange dreams.

"We told our dreams to a young Hebrew, slave to Captain of the guard, who told us exactly what our dreams meant. Everything he said did come to pass. Today I am serving you and the baker was executed, impaled upon a pole."

Pharaoh commands Potiphar be brought to him at once.

PHARAOH DEMANDS ANSWERS

"I want answers for my reoccurring dreams, Potiphar, and my butler tells me you have someone in your custody who can interpret dreams," Pharaoh says. Potiphar affirms to Pharaoh that reports of Joseph's ability to interpret dreams accurately are true.

Rumors fly around the royal palace place that a prison dream interpreter named Joseph will soon meet with Pharaoh.

POTIPHAR PREPARES JOSEPH

Early today, Potiphar released a Hebrew named Joseph from prison to get him ready for the high level meeting with Pharaoh.

Potiphar's hairdressers and valets are grooming Joseph with a shave, shower and cosmetic accents around his eyes.

Potiphar's personal valet dresses Joseph in elegantly tailored garments appropriate for his appearance before Pharaoh.

It is reported, that Potiphar and his palace guards are to escort Joseph to the Royal Palace for a high level meeting today.

PHARAOH'S DREAM SUMMIT

"I am looking for answers, Joseph," Pharaoh exclaims during a Dream summit meeting conducted at the Royal Palace with court sages, advisors and magicians in attendance.

"My Chief Butler tells me you have interpreted his dreams. Since none of my closest advisors have been able to tell me what my dreams mean I have called for you to resolve the matter of my mysterious nightly visions."

JOSEPH RELIES ON DIVINE FAVOR

The young Hebrew is humbled before Pharaoh as he states he cannot explain these dreams by himself.

Joseph informs Pharaoh that only Almighty God can provide the meaning of the dreams.

Pharaoh is noticeably taken back by Joseph's humility and his belief in Divine revelation.

PHARAOH'S NILE DREAM

Pharaoh is speaking publicly today to the young Hebrew, Joseph, telling him the following account of his first dream.

"I was standing upon the bank of the Nile River," Pharaoh stated, "All of a sudden seven fat healthy cows came out of the Nile and begin to graze along the shore.

Then out of the Nile come seven very skinny and scrawny cows. I have never seen such awful specimens.

The skinny cows ate up the fat cows and soon they were as skinny as before."

PHARAOH'S FIELD OF DREAMS

Pharaoh also tells Joseph about a second reoccurring dream where he is standing in the field of grains.

"In this dream there are seven heads of grain on one stalk and all seven heads are full and healthy. Suddenly out of the very same stalk there sprouts seven withered skinny heads of grain, whereupon the skinny heads swallow the fat heads.

I have told these dreams to my advisors and sages over and over. Not one of them can tell me what these dreams mean," says Pharaoh.

JOSEPH'S PARADOXICAL PREDICTIONS FOR PHARAOH

The young Hebrew dream interpreter and protégé of Potiphar stands confidently before Pharaoh today and reveals the real meaning of both of his recent dreams. It is a good news and bad news scenario and is contradictory or absurd to some observers at the session.

"During the next seven years Egypt will be very prosperous," Joseph tells Pharaoh. "The economy of the nation will flourish as never before.

However a dramatic change in climate conditions will bring about seven years of a very severe famine, resulting in food and grain shortages. Starvation will threaten the entire world."

DOUBLE DREAMS IMPACT

"Both dreams have the same message and have been sent from the Almighty," Joseph tells Pharaoh and his advisors.

"God is clearly telling you what will come to pass over the next 14 years in Egypt. Double trouble is just ahead and we must act now", Joseph warns Pharaoh.

DIRE WARNING CAUSES PANIC

"Drought and lack of storage facilities will threaten the national economy," states dream interpreter Joseph during his high level meeting with Pharaoh.

As the news spreads, hoarding begins quickly in some towns and cities and Pharaoh promises to take quick action to prevent economic chaos.

JOSEPH'S SAVING IDEAS

Joseph suggests to Pharaoh that he find someone to administer a nationwide agriculture program that would divide the country into five farm regions for royal storehouses to be constructed and administered. All excess crops of the next seven years will be stored for later use.

Under this strategy there will be enough to eat when the seven years of drought and famine come according to the young Hebrew dream reader. Failure to act now will bring about disaster Joseph tells Pharaoh.

EMERGENCY MEETING
CALLED BY PHARAOH

Pharaoh calls an emergency meeting with his advisors and administrative assistants today to deal with the predicted economic crises Joseph has foreseen in his series of curious dreams.

Pharaoh is seeking to find a leader to put in charge of a nationwide effort to increase per acre crop production and develop a nationwide network of food storage silos as soon as possible.

After meeting with his advisors Pharaoh plans to make a public announcement before the end of the day.

SERVE GOD BY SERVNG OTHERS

Joseph the dream interpreter is invited to the Royal Palace today for an agricultural planning summit.

"Here is a man who is clearly filled with the Spirit of God", says Pharaoh today after a meeting with his advisors who agreed with his choice. "Who can do this job better than you Joseph? "

"Since God revealed to you the meaning of my dreams, you are the wisest man in our land", Pharaoh continued. "I hereby appoint you to be Prince of Egypt over our economic recovery plan. You have full authority, Joseph and whatever you say must be done. Only I alone outrank you."

JOSEPH PREDICTS BUMPER CROPS

The Egyptian agricultural stock market takes off. Farmers get low interest government loans to buy new farming implements.

Some observers say Joseph is moving apace in his role as the nation's top agricultural post as the grain commodity market establishes a bumper crop.

Local Egyptian maidens at the Temple of Passionate Hours call Joseph a Dream Boat ready to lay anchor.

JOSEPH PROMOTED TO #2 BEHIND THE PHARAOH

The Young Hebrew Joseph is named second banana in the nation. Joseph's image appears on walls of teenage girl's rooms nationwide.

"Joseph the Dreamer" drawings dominate pop culture for 14 weeks.

The Dreamer makes the cover of 12 national cuneiform tablets.

SWEARING IN CEREMONY AT ROYAL PALACE

JOSEPH NAMED PRINCE

"Today I place you in charge of all the land of Egypt." Pharaoh states as he places his personal signet ring on the finger of Joseph.

At the Royal Palace anointing ceremonies Joseph kneels before Pharaoh as Pharaoh places an elegant handcrafted Royal Golden Chain around his neck before issuing the following proclamation to the nation: "I, the King of Egypt, swear that you will have complete charge over all the land of Egypt."

Joseph is now officially second in the chain of command with God like powers over Egypt's population and economy.

JOSEPH SEEN ON CHARIOT

Newly appointed Prince, 30 year old Joseph, travels nationwide conducting a series of town meetings.

Joseph's Chariot *Second In Command II* outruns everything on the road.

"KNEEL DOWN" SHOUTED OUT

Pharaoh commands that wherever Joseph travels, a royal pronouncement "Kneel down" will precede him.

Once an obscure Hebrew, Joseph is suddenly famous across the land.

Rumors are rampant that he once served time in jail for foul play. With the help of Potiphar, Joseph has been reinvented as a person with gravitas and great leadership skills.

JOSEPH'S POPULARITY SOARS

Wealthy Egyptians seek out Joseph for tips on which crops to grow for the best results.

More revelations about his vision for Egypt's economy are to be detailed along with an action plan for national prosperity.

A possible historical Monument deal is rumored to be in the works for the handsome young Hebrew.

Agriculture markets explode as farmers expand sowing their fields for greater harvests.

"ZAPHENATH-PANEAH"
JOSEPH'S NEW HANDLE

Today Pharaoh has decreed a new name for Joseph, an Egyptian name, Zaphenath-Paneah.

Joseph's new name means "He has the God-like power of life and death."

Joseph believes that it is his faith in God that has enabled him to re-invent his life and place him in a unique position of power and authority in a land of many Gods and Goddesses.

PHARAOH IS MATCH MAKER

Pharaoh announces the arrangement of the marriage of Asenath, daughter of Potiphera, high priest of the sun God Ra, and Zaphenath-Paneah also known as Joseph, Second in the Chain of Command.

MEDIA COVERS WEDDING

Asenath and Zaphenath-Paneah are voted best looking couple in Egypt as Asenath, daughter of Potiphera wears breathtaking golden garments made by the House of RA, exclusive clothiers to Pharaoh.

Egypt's most famous honeymoon couple has set sail on the Royal Barge headed for a secret destination away from adoring crowds.

Exclusive Asenath and Zaphenath-Paneah wedding drawings will be released to the public soon.

JOSEPH IS BACK TO WORK:
STORAGE SILO STOCKS SOAR:

Zaphenath-Paneah has authorized construction of 150,000 storage silos nationwide causing the price of bricks and straw to jump dramatically.

Brick layers are going on a work slowdown to try for higher wages.

Futures are forecasting bumper crops to sell at record prices due to government purchases by Zaphenath-Paneah.

PRINCE HOLDS
TOWN HALL MEETINGS

After meeting with Pharaoh, Prince Zaphenath-Paneah has scheduled more town hall meetings across the land.

The nation's second most powerful man will answer all questions regarding the new government agricultural program to stockpile grain.

Everything Zaphenath-Paneah learned from Potiphar and his father, Jacob, has equipped him for this assignment to galvanize the nation into action in order to save the world from famine and starvation.

It is a mind boggling challenge to Zaphenath-Paneah who often ponders about his family back in Cannon land and their situation during this difficult time. Is his father still alive?

PRINCE'S APPROVAL SURGES

Polls show a 98% approval rating for the former Hebrew slave named Joseph as hundreds of granaries are filled to the brim and overflowing.

Current *Ben Ben* opinion polls show that 99% of farmers back Joseph.

SUBSIDIES FOR AGRICULTURE

Zaphenath-Paneah encourages farmers to plant more crops and promises to buy everything they grow.

Farmers are reaping windfall profits by increasing their acreage under cultivation.

Everything the government subsidizes flourishes during this wave of growth.

GRANARIES ARE OVERFLOWING

Pharaoh's Prince has requisitioned a portion of every producing farm in the country increasing the cost of grain in the market place.

Bakers are passing on the increased cost of business to customers.

Farmer's plows and shears are in short supply as farm acreage expands. Farmers want to be part of helping to provide when the famine comes.

EGYPT'S GNP AT HISTORIC HIGH

Rich farmers flourish and expand as demand for their harvests increase year after year.

The highest productivity in decades brings the Gross National Product to historic highs and brings prosperity to the nation.

BREAD BASKET TO THE WORLD

A worldwide drought has resulted in food shortages everywhere but in Egypt which has planned ahead and has vast storage areas filled with grains and food stuffs.

Hundreds of people from surrounding nations are flooding into Egypt seeking to purchase food supplies. Daily crossings of hundreds of people are sighted along the Egyptian border as people seek refuge from starvation.

Border security is tightened by Zaphenath-Paneah as severe famine engulfs surrounding countries.

MIGRANTS SWARM BORDERS

Farm workers and housekeeping helpers from nearby Canaan nations are put to work in record numbers according to the

Department of Imported Slaves and Bond Servants.

Border Chariot Patrols are on full alert. Zaphenath-Paneah personally interviews many foreign immigrants coming into Egypt seeking grain and food.

ANNOUNCEMENT OF FIRST BORN

Asenath and Zaphenath-Paneah first born son is named Manasseh which translated means "Made To Forget." Asenath and Zaphenath-Paneah are proud of their first born.

Zaphenath-Paneah told the local paparazzi yesterday that this was God making up to him for all the bad and sad times of his youth.

SECOND SON ANNOUNCED

The nation's most popular couple Asenath and Zaphenath-Paneah name their second son Ephraim. The name means "fruitful." Zaphenath-Paneah says that the given name Ephraim also applies to his life "For God has made me fruitful in this land of my slavery."

The Egyptian Times reports hundreds of boys are been named Manasseh and Ephraim as revealed in recent birth records at the Nile Hall of Records.

CHAPTER 6 *REUNION*

FAMINE FORMENTS FEAR

Many surrounding countries are now experiencing crop failures, resulting in the worst famine in decades.   Lack of rainfall brings severe drought conditions and crop failures throughout the region.

Reports of food shortages have resulted in thousands of immigrants flocking to Egypt to beg for food.

Pharaoh's Royal Border patrol remains over worked and underpaid as horses are worn out pulling the chariots along the border.

EGYPT OPENS FOOD BANKS

With a severe famine all over the world, Zaphenath-Paneah announces the opening of Egypt's food banks nationwide to meet the increasing demand for food at home and abroad.

People from around the world are flocking to Egypt in growing numbers resulting in the cost of basic necessities to increase dramatically.

JACOB'S SONS OFF TO EGYPT

Facing starvation in the Land of Canaan, the elderly Patriarch Jacob has ordered his sons to travel to Egypt to buy grain and food supplies.

Because of the severe economic downturn Jacob decides to keep Joseph's younger brother Benjamin at home as he fears harm might come to him on the long journey due to high crime. He has already lost one son, Joseph, and the thought of losing another is stressful.

BROTHERS BLIND TO JOSEPH

Joseph's ten older brothers arrive in Egypt today seeking to purchase food because of the severe famine in Canaan.

Coming before Zaphenath-Paneah the brothers do not recognize their long "dead" brother as they bow down low with their faces on the ground.

Joseph instantly recognizes the new arrivals from Canaan.

JOSEPH'S ICY WELCOME

While his brothers bow low before him, Joseph instantly recalls his childhood dreams of brothers bowing before him as well as his brother's reactions upon hearing his dream.

Speaking Egyptian through an interpreter to his brothers as Prince Zaphenath-Paneah, he interrogates them coldly.

"Where are you from? Why are you here?" Joseph asks them. The brothers reply that they are from Canaan and are seeking to buy food.

SPIES FROM CANAAN JAILED

Egypt's Prince has 10 suspicious travelers from Canaan arrested today accusing them of spying. The alleged spies deny the charges claiming to be just a band of brothers seeking food for their father, younger brother and families back in Canaan land.

Zaphenath-Paneah tells them they will be held in prison until their younger brother is brought to Egypt to confirm their story.

As they are being locked up, Zaphenath-Paneah states he might consider releasing one of them to travel back to Canaan to bring their brother.

AN OFFER THEY CAN'T REFUSE

After three days behind bars, the 10 Hebrew travelers from Canaan are brought before their brother Joseph, now governor over Egypt.

"Being a God fearing man, I have decided to give you all a chance to prove your honesty," Joseph states, "and therefore, I have decided to free all of you except for Simeon who will remain behind until you all return."

REGRETTING THE PAST

As the foreign refuges from Canaan hear the offer from Prince Zaphenath-Paneah they begin whispering among themselves in Hebrew that all this was happening to them now because of what they did to Joseph so many years ago. "We are being repaid for our selfishness and evil" Reuben said. "Didn't I tell you not to harm Joseph? But you all did not listen to me."

"We saw our brother's terror and we did not listen to his pleas and now we are going to die because we murdered Joseph", they murmured among themselves.

The Hebrew bothers do not know the bi-lingual Egyptian Prince standing before them is in fact their own brother and is able to understand their regrets and anxiety.

JOSEPH'S EXISTENTIAL MOMENT

Zaphenath-Paneah abruptly departs from his heated meeting with the Hebrew prisoners today at the country's top security prison.

Once behind closed doors, insiders say later that the young Prince of Egypt had a severe emotional breakdown.

JOSEPH'S CHILDHOOD TRAMA

Confronting the delegation of Hebrews from Canaan Land, Joseph relives the vivid memories of his brother's taunts and torture, being tossed down into a dry well and sold into slavery.

His years of separation from his family, being sold as a slave and years of imprisonment for something he did not do, flood his mind causing uncontrollable anguish for a short while.

JOSEPH'S GOD GIVEN PURPOSE

The young Prince suddenly realizes that what his brothers did to him for evil, ultimately resulted in his rising up to become almost the most powerful man in the world. What was done with evil intent has put him in a position to rescue his feuding family from starvation.

Reflecting back Joseph gains a new perspective and appreciation about the significance of his putting his faith and trust in God, day by day, hour by hour, minute by minute, throughout his life.

Joseph accepts that all that happened throughout his life was not an accident but was part of God's ultimate purpose for his life. Regaining his perspective, Joseph is now ready to face his brothers fully composed and ready to launch a daring plan to bring his family to Egypt. He has served others, now he is determined to unite his family as well as save them from starvation.

JOSEPH'S CLEVER CASH CAMPAIGN

Joseph instructs his staff to fill the saddle sacks of his brother's animals with grain. He then directs that they covertly return each brother's cash payment by hiding it amidst their supplies for the return trip home to Canaan.

GOOD/BAD NEWS FOR JACOB

Back in Canaan Jacob's sons discover that all the money they had paid for the grain is inside each food container.

Jacob is told that they had to leave Simeon behind in jail in order for them to be able to return home.

In addition they have to report to Jacob that they cannot return to Egypt without bringing young Benjamin. This request causes deep dismay for Jacob who fears losing another son. Much pain and guilt is felt by the brothers as they remember their bad deed.

JACOB'S REAL ANGST

Seeking famine relief once again, Jacob prepares his sons to return to Egypt for supplies. Jacob gathers gifts of honey, spices, almonds, pistachio nuts and doubles the money required for payment of grain hoping to placate the Egyptian Governor.

Reluctantly, a fearful Jacob allows Benjamin to make the journey. He knows he will have many sleepless nights of worry ahead until Benjamin returns.

CASH REFUNDS REFUSED!

Upon reaching the Palace gate, the brothers attempt to return the money they found hidden in their sacks.

Zaphenath-Paneah's current manager reassures them that it is not necessary because "Your God must have put it there for we did receive your cash payment." They are dumbfounded and confused.

The household manager then has their hostage brother Simeon released to rejoin them for an upcoming Royal banquet.

ROYAL ACTION CAUSES CONCERN

Upon their return to Egypt, the sons of Jacob stand once again before Joseph also known as Prince Zaphenath-Paneah. Speaking in Egyptian he instructs his manager to take his brothers to his palace for the noon meal.

As the brothers approach the Royal compound they worry that they are headed for trouble because of the money they found in their grain sacks after their first trip. It must be paid!

BOWING TO A ROYAL PRINCE

Prince Zaphenath-Paneah extends his hospitality to his distant family members with a lavish welcoming feast.

The brothers bow low and present their father's gifts and introduce their younger brother Benjamin. Joseph ponders the fulfillment of another one of his childhood dreams.

Joseph inquires about their father, Jacob. They respond "He is alive and well." And they bow before him again.

Joseph once again remembers his childhood dreams of his brothers bowing low before him and quickly takes leave of the group.

A FABULOUS FAMILY FEAST

Prince Zaphenath-Paneah sits alone at the Royal head table. Meanwhile, his brothers are seated nearby, totally apart from Egyptian guests whose racial profiling causes them to despise Hebrews.

Joseph has his brothers served food and wine from his table with extra VIP service for young Benjamin who is the center of attention.

Joseph gives his favors to his younger brother Benjamin and gives him his blessings before retiring behind closed doors to hide his deep emotions at seeing him after so many years.

JOSEPH AN EMOTIONAL MESS

Childhood dreams flood his memory as Joseph watches his brothers bow low before him, causing him to retreat to regain his composure.

Finally getting his emotions under control Joseph calmly and confidently returns to his anxiously waiting brothers. The Royal Prince of Egypt invites his estranged brothers to follow him into the royal dining room. They trail after the Prince of Egypt while still wondering among themselves what in the world is about to happen.

DEPARTING DECEPTION

The night before his brothers are to depart for home, Joseph instructs his manager to fill each of their sacks with grain and once again to covertly place back in each person's sack the money they had paid for the food.

At Joseph's direction, his precious silver cup is to be placed into Benjamin's grain sack along with his money. Joseph has hatched a plan to get his father Jacob to come to Egypt.

STOP THIEVES!

Jacob's sons are stopped by Joseph's household manager shortly after leaving the city at dawns early light.

At Joseph's instructions, the manager asks them why they have stolen the Royal Prince's personal silver drinking cup. The brothers deny stealing anything.

"If you find the Prince's special drinking cup with any one of us, we will let the guilty person be executed for stealing and we will be slaves forever to your master," was a brother's response.

The household manager replied quietly that only the guilty person would become a slave and as for the rest they will be free to depart the land.

TO CATCH A THIEF

The manager, as he was instructed by Joseph, searches each sack starting with the eldest brother. Anxiety increases as the search moves from brother to brother down to the youngest.

No silver cup is discovered until the manager finally removes it from Benjamin's sack just where he had placed it in the first place.

PRINCE CONFRONTS HIS BROTHERS

Returning to the Royal Palace, Joseph's brothers fall face down on the ground before him.

"What in the world were you thinking?" asks Joseph.

"Did you not know that I would know who it was that would dare steal from me?" he asked them.

BROTHER'S PROCLAIM INNOCENCE

Judah, speaking for the brothers, said "How can we prove our innocence? For it seems that God is punishing us for our sins. We are here to all become your slaves."

THIEF TO REMAIN IN JAIL

The Prince waves his hands to the assembled brothers saying only the thief who stole his prized possession would remain in custody. The rest of the brothers were free to return home to their father.

JOSEPH HEARS HIS STORY

Judah pleads with Joseph on behalf of their aging father Jacob who he says will die if Benjamin does not return home with them.

He tells the Prince of Egypt the story of Jacobs's two youngest sons. And how one of them, Joseph, disappeared forever and was most likely torn to pieces by wild beasts. The loss of his son put their father into a deep depression for years.

"I promised my father I would watch over Benjamin and would bring him safely back home. How shall I return home to my father if my younger brother is not with me? I cannot bear the thought of what this might do to him to lose another son."

Joseph's love and admiration for his father had sustained him during his years of captivity in Egypt and he is now deeply touched upon hearing Judah's heart felt plea for their father.

RIVETING ROYAL REDEMPTORY REACTION RESONATES

After hearing his older brother Judah's heart rendering story, the Royal Prince commands all attendants and servants to leave the room in order that he might speak privately to the prisoners in his custody.

The brothers huddled together expecting the worst was about to unfold.

ZAPHENATH-PANEAHA IS JOSEPH

"I AM JOSEPH!" Time stands still today behind closed doors in the Palace of Prince Zaphenath-Paneah.

Standing before his trembling brothers, the second most powerful man in the world announces to them that he is in fact their long lost brother, Joseph.

Shocked and stunned with disbelief, Joseph's brothers slowly gather around Egypt's second most powerful person who announces to them that he is in fact their long missing and believed dead brother.

There was total silence until the Prince spoke these words:

"I am your brother whom you sold into slavery in Egypt."

The brothers could not believe their eyes or ears and stand tongue tied into shocked silence. This cannot be the brother they sold into slavery years ago. This was just too fantastic to be true. Their long lost brother is standing before them announcing that he is the ruler over Egypt!

JOSEPH'S POSTIVE ATTITUDE

A very emotional Joseph tells his brothers "Do not be distressed because you sold me into slavery because God sent me here to keep you and your families alive so that you can become part of a great nation."

"God took me from slavery to jail but then elevated me to become an advisor to Pharaoh and a ruler over all of Egypt."

"The evil you meant to do to me, God turned into something good. I was sent ahead to protect and preserve our family."

GOD'S STUNNING SYNCHRONICITY

Joseph tells his brothers "It is God who sent me here to Egypt, not you. God has made me chief advisor to Pharaoh and Governor of the entire nation."

Joseph embraces each brother, one by one, asking that they hurry back to Jacob and bring him and their families back to Egypt where all may live in Goshen and be near the Prince.

Breaking news from the Royal Palace:

REUNION ROCKS BROTHERS

The Royal Palace is the scene of an emotional reunion for Zaphenath-Paneah as he has a closed door meeting with his brothers. Loud cries and weeping are heard throughout the palace.

It does not take long for the news of the family reunion to reach the ears of Pharaoh.

It has been revealed that Prince Zaphenath-Paneah is in fact the long missing son of the Hebrew Patriarch, Jacob.

PHARAOH BREAKS HIS SILENCE

A very happy Pharaoh meets with Joseph today and requests that his brothers return immediately to Canaan and bring back their father and families to Egypt to reside in Goshen land.

Pharaoh has commanded that transportation and provisions will be provided for Joseph's brothers return trip to Canaan land.

FIVE MORE YEARS OF FAMINE

"The drought will become more severe", Joseph says, "Therefore everyone must come to Egypt immediately."

"Hurry back to my father and tell him, your son Joseph says, God has made me chief of all the land of Egypt. Come to me right away!"

"YOU WILL LIVE OFF
THE FAT OF THE LAND!"

An emotional Pharaoh commands Joseph to tell his brothers that he will assign them to the best territory in all of Egypt.

Pharaoh himself is providing wagons and provisions for the journey back to Canaan in order to bring their father and families back to live in Goshen, a land flowing with milk and honey.

BROTHER'S EXTREME MAKEOVER

Joseph has outfitted each of his brothers with finest Egyptian garments and shoes.

For his youngest brother Benjamin, Joseph orders five changes of hand tailored clothing. In addition he has given the young lad 300 silver coins as traveling money.

JOSEPH'S LAVISH FAMILY GIFTS

Joseph is shipping 10 donkey loads of gifts from Egypt to his father Jacob as well as 10 donkey loads of grain, food and good things to feed his extended family in Canaan.

PRINCE'S PARTING WORDS

The last thing Joseph tells his brothers is, "Don't quarrel along the way!" He knows his brothers pretty well, even after all these years, it would seem.

He says the family is whole again and they are to rejoice and not fight among themselves as he urges them to bring his father and extended family back to relocate in Egypt.

JOSEPH IS ALIVE AND WELL!

When the sons of Jacob arrive home in Canaan land they shout the fantastic and amazing news to their elderly father Jacob that his long lost son Joseph is indeed not only alive but is a ruler over all of Egypt.

JACOB IS IN A STATE OF SHOCK

Dumbfounded and bowled over by the news, the fabled Canaan Patriarch Jacob cannot believe that his long dead son is not only alive but is a ruler in Egypt, the most powerful nation on earth.

Jacob's mind spins with distant memories of his long missing favorite son.

JACOB'S LATE NIGHT DREAM

During the night Jacob hears the voice of God speaking to him in his dreams, fear not going to Egypt.

"I will go down with you into Egypt and I will bring your descendants back again. You will die in Egypt with Joseph at your side."

With these words of reassurance in his mind, Jacob sends Judah ahead to tell Joseph they are on their way to Goshen.

GIFTS ARRIVE IN CANAAN

When the wagons and donkeys bearing gifts from Prince Joseph arrive in Canaan his elderly father Jacob breaks down and weeps for joy, finally accepting the fact that Joseph truly lives.

HEART WARMING REUNION

When Jacob sees his son Joseph riding toward him on his Royal Chariot, his heart pounds in his chest, his mind floods with memories of his long dead son who is alive and coming toward him.

The two meet and embrace, weeping emotionally for some time as did most family members surrounding father and son.

Jacob clings to Joseph crying, "My son, my son...."

PROPER PROTOCAL PLEASES PHARAOH

Joseph briefs his brothers so they will be prepared for their upcoming meeting with the Pharaoh.

"Pharaoh will ask you about your work and so you must be prepared to answer that you are shepherds," Joseph says. "This is vital because traditionally shepherds are despised and hated in certain places in Egypt. However, when Pharaoh learns being shepherds is our family tradition, he will grant you high end property in Egypt."

HIGH LEVEL PHARAOH SUMMIT

Prince Zaphenath-Paneah, also known as Joseph, brings five of his brothers to meet his Royal Majesty Pharaoh at a welcoming Summit at the Royal Palace.

Today, Joseph's family petitions Pharaoh for the right to remain in Egypt as they have brought all of their families and possessions with them including their flocks and herds.

JOSEPH'S FAMILY
TO RESIDE IN GOSHEN

After a historic summit meeting with Pharaoh today, Prince Zaphenath-Paneah announces that his father, Patriarch Jacob of Canaan Land, and his brothers and their families, have been given title to some of the best pasture land in Goshen, Egypt, as home for their livestock farm. Pharaoh puts Joseph's brothers in charge of his own flocks.

JACOB BLESSES PHARAOH

During a private meeting with Pharaoh, 130 year old Jacob, father of Prince Zaphenath-Paneah, gives his blessing to Pharaoh upon meeting him and again just before departing the Royal Palace.

CHAPTER 8 *THE PLAN*

PHARAOH'S STIMULOUS PLAN

As the economic crises dramatically increases, the people in both Canaan and Egypt are reported to be starving.

Pharaoh responds by developing a stimulus plan for Joseph to administer with the assistance of hundreds of government assistants and bookkeepers.

Joseph, #2 in Egypt, will implement Pharaoh's three step plan for rescue and recovery.

JOSEPH PROVIDES DETAILS ON THREE-STEP PLAN

Joseph reveals the plan.

Phase one:

Joseph will collect all the cash in Egypt and Canaan in exchange for food.

Pharaoh's governmental treasury houses are starting to burst at the seams.

Phase two:

Joseph will buy everyone's sheep and cattle in exchange for food.

Phase three:

Joseph will purchase all the land.

Some observers worry about rising prices for grain, livestock and land after hearing Joseph's game plan.

REAL ESTATE & LIVESTOCK PRICES
SOAR IN BULL MARKET

The cost of land and livestock in Egypt continues to rise as the government buys everything in sight.

Top dollar is paid by the Royal Treasury under the control of Joseph, the only man in the country able to manage the crises, according to Pharaoh.

"Joseph is the only one in the entire country that can handle our economic crises," says Pharaoh.

JOSEPH'S RESCUE & RECOVERY
PLAN IMPLEMENTED

Under Joseph's direction all horses, goats, sheep and other livestock in Egypt and Canaan are now owned by the government.

Joseph continues to buy all the land as the severe famine crises rises. People are left with no choice but to sell.

Critics say Pharaoh will soon own everything and everybody.

PHARAOH'S CRONIES GET
SPECIAL TREATMENT

The only land not purchased by Joseph is land belonging to Pharaoh's personal priests.

Joseph says that he does not need to buy the priests' properties because priests are assigned food from Pharaoh and therefore there was no need for them to sell.

EVERYBODY AND EVERYTHING OWNED BY PHARAOH

Joseph implements a New Deal Land Investment and Recovery Act.

Former land owners will receive seed to sow. One fifth of everything harvested will belong to Pharaoh.

The remaining harvest is to be used to plant the next harvest and as food for farm labor.

PHARAOH POLLS HIGHEST EVER

Man on the street poll reveals Pharaoh has a 98% approval rating.

Most people say they are glad to work for the Pharaoh as he and Joseph saved their lives.

RISE OF THE NANNY STATE

Pharaoh announces his government will take care of everyone, from cradle to the grave and beyond, including the life hereafter.

PHARAOH'S MEDIA BLITZ

Images of Pharaoh sprout up across the nation and in foreign countries who are seeking food subsidies from the Royal Silos and warehouses.

20% TAX ON ALL CROPS

The law of the land is 20% tax on all new crops produced except for those on land owned by Priests of Pharaoh.

It seems the Royal government is exempt from the policies the population at large must obey or be jailed if they do not obey.

PROSPERITY, POPULATION SOAR

There is a growing "silver lining" in Egypt's business climate, as Prince Joseph's family is prospering greatly since settling on some of the nation's most fertile soil in the land of Goshen.

During the past 17 years since the family arrived there has also been a population explosion in Jacob's extended family.

DEATH BED ADOPTION

Prince Joseph arrives in Goshen with his two sons Manasseh and Ephraim to visit his bed ridden half-blind father Jacob.

During an emotional visit, Patriarch Jacob says to Joseph, "I never thought I would see you again, but now God has let me see your children too."

During the visit, Jacob adopts both sons of Joseph to insure their inheritance in Canaan.

JACOB'S FINAL BLESSING UPSETTING

Jacobs's greater blessing on the youngest son of Joseph, Ephraim, causes anxiety for Prince Joseph who tells his father his hands are on the wrong son.

However, Jacob tells Joseph he knows what he is doing. Manasseh will become a great man, but his young brother shall become even greater.

His final blessing on the two boys concluded with "May the people of Israel bless each other by saying, 'God make you as prosperous as Ephraim and Manasseh."

JACOB SEES THE FUTURE

During his last meeting with his 12 sons, Jacob forecasts what he sees for each one of them.

As always his most bountiful blessing was for Joseph who has overcome persecution and slavery.

JOSEPH'S FATHER DIES

It was almost two decades ago when the well-known Hebrew Patriarch Jacob, also called Israel, was welcomed to Egypt by Pharaoh. Jacob died in his sleep at the age of 147 years.

Father to 12 sons, including Prince Joseph, Jacob, while wealthy in land and livestock, was most of all a dedicated family man who loved his many sons and grandchildren. He especially favored his famous son, Joseph. His final request to Joseph was that he be buried near his father

Isaac and his wife Rebekah in the Land of Canaan.

DAY OF MOURNING

Joseph orders Jacob's 40 day embalming process and national mourning, covering 70 days, to begin tonight.

Rumors abound that Joseph will not bury his father in Egypt but will take his remains to the Land of Canaan to the family burial plot.

Pharaoh orders a national period of mourning as Joseph's father Jacob transitions into the afterlife across the Nile River.

Pharaoh permits Joseph to leave Egypt to return his Father to Canaan land.

JACOB BURIED IN CANAAN

Joseph leads a large delegation of Pharaoh's counselors and assistants as well as senior officers of Egypt to the Land of Canaan to his father's burial site, the cave of Machpelah.

A huge gathering attends the solemn funeral memorial service followed by seven days of mourning.

RIP PATRIARCH JACOB

Local residents of the village of Atad are moved by the profound and deep mourning by the Egyptians and rename the village Abel-mizraim, which translates means: Egyptian Mourners.

Jacob is placed in his final resting place entombed in the cave of Machpelah.

Village leaders forecast a huge flow of tourists into the town in the months ahead.

Cave Machpelah, originally purchased by Abraham, is now a famous landmark drawing visitors from around the nation.

"FEAR NOT" JOSEPH
SAYS TO HIS BROTHERS

It is reported that Joseph's brothers have begged his forgiveness for the evil they did to him.

"Fear not," Joseph has said to them, "What you meant for evil God meant for good."

Joseph spoke with kindly reassurances that all would be well with his brothers and their families.

EXCLUSIVE:

JOSEPH'S DEATH BED PROMISE

Reliable sources report that the famed, second most famous person in Egypt, Joseph, predicted upon his death bed that his descendants someday would be taken back to the land promised to Abraham, Isaac and Jacob.

JOSEPH DIES

Joseph died yesterday at age 110. He will be embalmed and buried in a royal coffin in Egypt.

Joseph's brothers vow before God that one day Joseph's bones will be taken with them when God leads them out of Egypt.

FUTURE EPILOGUE HEADLINES:

HEBREW NATION A THREAT

Startling statistics reveal Hebrew immigrants have multiplied rapidly since the death of Joseph.

Latest census reports that Egypt's Goshen territory is dominated by Hebrews who arrived years ago during an economic depression made worse by bad government policies.

PHARAOH'S IRON FIST REVEALED

The new Pharaoh has no ties to Joseph or his family and has taken control of the highest office in the land with bold new polices in mind.

Pharaoh issues an executive order to all taskmasters to take over and manage the Hebrew labor work force.

Pharaoh fears the Hebrew invaders will take over the country and has sealed the nation's borders.

PHARAOH'S NEW LABOR POLICY

Effective immediately Pharaoh orders that all Hebrews residing in Egypt are to be under the control of the central government.

Government assigned Taskmasters will regulate and manage all Hebrew workers who hence forth have no legal standing before Pharaoh except to do as he commands.

TASKMASTERS INCREASE WORK LOAD OF HEBREWS

Hebrew workers work overtime to build city facilities in Pithom and Raamses.

To the dismay of the Pharaoh, Hebrew birth rates sky rocket even as working conditions reduce Hebrews into virtual slaves working long and hard.

PHARAOH SUPPORTS INFANTICIDE

Pharaoh has made it official; midwives are to murder all Hebrew newborn boys.

The public is encouraged to throw any newborn Hebrew baby into the river Nile.

EPILOGUE

LESSONS LEARNED FROM JOSEPH'S INNER DIRECTED LIFE:

Core principles enabled Joseph to be a servant of God and to follow his dreams.

JOSEPH'S CHALLENGES & RESPONSE

Tossed into a hole in the ground by his own brothers and then later sold into slavery did not alter Joseph's firm belief that God was with him.

JOSEPH THE POSSIBILITY DREAMER

Joseph was a possibility thinker, no matter what was happening in the circumstances or changing events of the moment around him he stayed true to his God and his beliefs.

He stayed positive through very tough times.

Often held in slavery or captivity, Joseph served his fellow man confident that God was with him as he hustled to make his dreams a reality.

JOSEPH'S SPIRITUAL GPS GUIDED HIM

Joseph's inner directed life guided him through all the external circumstances and events that altered his life unexpectedly. His internal moral compass was faith in a just and holy God.

God's Purpose is Service was the lifestyle Joseph lived by.

Joseph's faith in God engendered his high ethical standards early in life and shaped his passion to serve humanity to the best of his ability.

Joseph's story is about transparency and truthfulness. Early in life he learned to be honest with himself and others.

He was proactive and took responsibility for acquiring learned lessons from his experiences and by always choosing a positive, life affirming response to dire circumstances.

Early in life, Joseph learned time tested sound principles while working on his father's farm. Joseph's principled thinking empowered his honesty, duty, service and problem solving skills.

Joseph believed his life purpose was service to God.

Joseph believed that in serving others he was serving God.

His life of service to others helped to mold his character and shape his choices and options in life.

This humble personality is what made him a great leader.

However, this did not necessarily mean he always made the right choices in what was best for the people.

The unfolding story of Joseph's heirs 400 years later continues in the land of Egypt with historical headline stories of Moses:

Prince of Egypt
Deliverer, Lawgiver, Nation builder

www.ingramcontent.com/pod-product-compliance
Lightning Source LLC
Chambersburg PA
CBHW061138200626
46817CB00016B/2035